Doctor Birch and His Young Friends by William Makepeace Thackeray

Writing as M. A. Titmarsh

The great author of Vanity Fair and The Luck Of Barry Lyndon was born in India in 1811.

At age 5 his father died and his mother sent him back to England. His education was of the best but he himself seemed unable to apply his talents to a rigorous work ethic.

However, once he harnessed his talents the works flowed in novels, articles, short stories, sketches and lectures.

Sadly, his personal life was rather more difficult. After a few years of marriage his wife began to suffer from depression and over the years became detached from reality. Thackeray himself suffered from ill health later in his life and the one pursuit that kept him moving forward was that of writing. In his life time, he was placed second only to Dickens. High praise indeed.

Index of Contents

DOCTOR BIRCH

THE DOCTOR AND HIS STAFF

There is no need to say why I became Assistant Master and Professor of the English and French languages, flower-painting, and the German flute, in Doctor Birch's Academy, at Rodwell Regis. Good folks may depend on this that there was good reason for my leaving lodgings near London, and a genteel society, for an under-master's desk in that old school. I promise you, the fare at the Usher's table, the getting up at five o'clock in the morning, the walking out with little boys in the fields, (who used to play me tricks, and never could be got to respect my awful and responsible character as teacher in the school,) Miss Birch's vulgar insolence, Jack Birch's glum condescension, and the poor old Doctor's patronage, were not matters in themselves pleasurable: and that that patronage and those dinners were sometimes cruel hard to swallow. Never mind—my connexion with the place is over now, and I hope they have got a more efficient under-master.

Jack Birch (Rev. J. Birch, of St. Neot's Hall, Oxford,) is partner with his father the Doctor, and takes some of the classes. About his Greek I can't say much; but I will construe him in Latin any day. A more supercilious little prig, (giving himself airs, too, about his cousin, Miss Baby, who lives with the Doctor,) a more empty pompous little coxcomb I never saw. His white neckcloth looked as if it choked him. He used to try and look over that starch upon me and Prince the assistant, as if we were a couple of footmen. He didn't do much business in the school; but occupied his time in writing sanctified letters to the boys' parents, and in composing dreary sermons to preach to them.

The real master of the school is Prince; an Oxford man too: shy, haughty, and learned; crammed with Greek and a quantity of useless learning; uncommonly kind to the small boys; pitiless with the fools and the braggarts: respected of all for his honesty, his learning, his bravery, (for he hit out once in a boat-row in a way which astonished the boys and the bargemen,) and for a latent power about him, which all saw and confessed somehow. Jack Birch could never look him in the face. Old Miss Z. dared not put off any of her airs upon him. Miss Rosa made him the lowest of curtsies. Miss Raby said she was afraid of him. Good old Prince! many a pleasant night we have smoked in the Doctor's harness-room, whither we retired when our boys were gone to bed, and our cares and canes put by.

After Jack Birch had taken his degree at Oxford—a process which he effected with great difficulty—this place, which used to be called "Birch's," "Dr. Birch's Academy," and what not, became suddenly "Archbishop Wigsby's College of Rodwell Regis." They took down the old blue board with the gold letters, which has been used to mend the pig-stye since. Birch had a large school-room run up in the Gothic taste, with statuettes, and a little belfry, and a bust of Archbishop Wigsby in the middle of the school. He put the six senior boys into caps and gowns, which had rather a good effect as the lads sauntered down the street of the town, but which certainly provoked the contempt and hostility of the bargemen; and so great was his rage for academic costumes and ordinances, that he would have put me myself into a lay gown, with red knots and fringes, but that I flatly resisted, and said that a writing-master had no business with such paraphernalia.

By the way, I have forgotten to mention the Doctor himself. And what shall I say of him? Well, he has a very crisp gown and bands, a solemn air, a tremendous loud voice, and a grand and solemn air with the boys' parents, whom he receives in a study, covered round with the best bound books, which imposes upon many—upon the women especially—and makes them fancy that this is a Doctor indeed. But, Law bless you! He never reads the books; or opens one of them, except that in which he keeps his bands—and a Dugdale's Monasticon, which looks like a book, but is in reality a cupboard, where he has his almond cakes, and decanter of port wine. He gets up his classics with translations, or what the boys call cribs. They pass wicked tricks upon him when he hears the forms. The elder wags go to his study, and ask him to help them in hard bits of Herodotus or Thucydides: he says he will look over the passage, and flies for refuge to Mr. Prince, or to the crib.

He keeps the flogging department in his own hands; finding that his son was too savage. He has awful brows and a big voice. But his roar frightens nobody. It is only a lion's skin, or, so to say, a muff.

Little Mordant made a picture of him with large ears, like a well-known domestic animal, and had his own justly boxed for the caricature. The Doctor discovered him in the fact, and was in a flaming rage, and threatened whipping at first; but in the course of the day an opportune basket of game arriving from Mordant's father, the Doctor became mollified, and has burnt the picture with the ears. However I have one wafered up in my desk by the hand of the same little rascal: and the frontispiece of this very book is drawn from it.

THE COCK OF THE SCHOOL

I am growing an old fellow—and have seen many great folks in the course of my travels and time—Louis Philippe coming out of the Tuileries, His Majesty the King of Prussia and the Reichsverweser accolading each other, at Cologne, at my elbow; Admiral Sir Charles Napier (in an omnibus once), the Duke of Wellington, the immortal Goethe at Weimar, the late benevolent Pope Gregory XVI., and a score more of the famous in this world—the whom, whenever one looks at, one has a mild shock of awe and tremor. I like this feeling and decent fear and trembling with which a modest spirit salutes a Great Man.

Well, I have seen Generals capering on horseback at the head of their crimson battalions; Bishops sailing down cathedral aisles, with downcast eyes, pressing their trencher caps to their hearts with their fat white hands; College heads when her Majesty is on a visit; the Doctor in all his glory at the head of his school on Speech-day, a great sight,—and all great men these.

I have never met the late Mr. Thomas Cribb, but I have no doubt should have regarded him with the same feeling of awe with which I look every day at George Champion, the cock of Dr. Birch's school.

When, I say, I reflect as I go up and set him a sum, that he could whop me in two minutes, double up Prince and the other assistant, and pitch the Doctor out of window, I can't but think how great, how generous, how magnanimous a creature this is, that sits quite quiet and good-natured, and works his equation, and ponders through his Greek play. He might take the schoolroom pillars and pull the house down if he liked. He might close the door, and demolish every one of us like Antar, the lover of Ibla; but he lets us live. He never thrashes anybody without a cause, when woe betide the tyrant or the sneak!

I think that to be strong, and able to whop everybody,—(not to do it, mind you, but to feel that you were able to do it,)—would be the greatest of all gifts. There is a serene good humour which plays about George Champion's broad face, which shows the consciousness of this power, and lights up his honest blue eyes with a magnanimous calm.

He is invictus. Even when a cub there was no beating this lion. Six years ago the undaunted little warrior actually stood up to Frank Davison,—(the Indian officer now—poor little Charley's brother, whom Miss Raby nursed so affectionately,)—then seventeen years old, and the cock of Birch's. They were obliged to drag off the boy, and Frank, with admiration and regard for him, prophesied the great things he would do. Legends of combats are preserved fondly in schools; they have stories of such at Rodwell Regis, performed in the old Doctor's time, forty years ago.

Champion's affair with the Young Tutbury Pet, who was down here in training,—with Black the Bargeman,—with the three head boys of Doctor Wapshot's academy, whom he caught maltreating an outlying day-boy of ours, &c.,—are known to all the Rodwell Regis men. He was always victorious. He is modest and kind, like all great men. He has a good, brave, honest understanding. He cannot make verses like young Pinder, or read Greek like Lawrence the Prefect, who is a perfect young abyss of learning, and knows enough, Prince says, to furnish any six first-class men; but he does his work in a sound, downright way, and he is made to be the bravest of soldiers, the best of country parsons, an honest English gentleman wherever he may go.

Like all great men, George is good-humoured and lazy. There is a particular bench in the play-ground on which he will loll for hours on half-holidays, and is so affable that the smallest boys come and speak to him. It is pleasant to see the young cubs frisking round the honest lion. His chief friend and attendant, however, is young Jack Hall, whom he saved when drowning, out of the Miller's Pool. The attachment of the two is curious to witness. The smaller lad gambolling, playing tricks round the bigger one, and perpetually making fun of his protector. They are never far apart, and of holidays you may meet them miles away from the school. George sauntering heavily down the lanes with his big stick, and little Jack larking with the pretty girls in the cottage windows.

George has a boat on the river, in which, however, he commonly lies smoking, whilst Jack sculls him. He does not play at cricket, except when the school plays the county, or at Lord's in the holidays. The boys can't stand his bowling, and when he hits, it is like trying to catch a cannon-ball. I have seen him at tennis. It is a splendid sight to behold the young fellow bounding over the court with streaming yellow hair, like young Apollo in a flannel jacket.

The other head boys are Lawrence the Captain, Bunce, famous chiefly for his magnificent appetite, and Pitman, sur-named Roscius, for his love of the drama. Add to these Swanky, called Macassar, from his partiality to that condiment, and who has varnished boots, wears white gloves on Sundays, and looks out for Miss Pinkerton's school (transferred from Chiswick to Rodwell Regis, and conducted by the nieces of the late Miss Barbara Pinkerton, the friend of Our Great Lexicograplier, upon the principles approved by him and practised by that admirable woman,) as it passes into church.

Representations have been made concerning Mr. Horace Swanky's behaviour; rumours have been uttered about notes in verse, conveyed in three-cornered puffs, by Mrs. Buggies, who serves Miss Pinkerton's young ladies on Fridays—and how Miss Didow, to whom the tart and enclosure were addressed, tried to make away with herself by swallowing a ball of cotton. But I pass over these absurd reports, as likely to affect the reputation of an admirable Seminary conducted by irreproachable females. As they go into church (Miss P. driving in her flock of lambkins with the crook of her parasol,) how can it be helped if her forces and ours sometimes collide, as the boys are on their way up to the organ-loft? And I don't believe a word about the three-cornered puff, but rather that it was the invention of that jealous Miss Birch, who is jealous of Miss Raby, jealous of everybody who is good and handsome, and who has her own ends in view, or I am very much in error.

THE LITTLE SCHOOL-ROOM

What they call the little school-room is a small room at the other end of the great school; through which you go to the Doctor's private house, and where Miss Raby sits with her pupils. She has a half-dozen very small ones over whom she presides and teaches them in her simple way, until they are big or learned enough to face the great school-room. Many of them are in a hurry for promotion, the graceless little simpletons, and know no more than their elders when they are well off.

She keeps the accounts, writes out the bills, superintends the linen and sews on the general shirt-buttons. Think of having such a woman at home to sew on one's shirt-buttons! But peace, peace, thou foolish heart!

Miss Raby is the Doctor's niece. Her mother was a beauty (quite unlike old Zoe therefore); and she married a pupil in the old Doctor's time, who was killed afterwards, a Captain in the East India service, at the siege of Bhurtpore. Hence a number of Indian children come to the Doctor's, for Raby was very much liked, and the uncle's kind reception of the orphan has been a good speculation for the school-keeper.

It is wonderful how brightly and gaily that little quick creature does her duty. She is the first to rise, and the last to sleep, if any business is to be done. She sees the other two women go off to parties in the town without even so much as wishing to join them. It is Cinderella, only contented to stay at home—content to bear Zoe's scorn and to admit Flora's superior charms,—and to do her utmost to repay her uncle for his great kindness in housing her.

So, you see, she works as much as three maid-servants for the wages of one. She is as thankful when the Doctor gives her a new gown, as if he had presented her with a fortune: laughs at his stories most good-humouredly, listens to Zoe's scolding most meekly, admires Flora with all her heart, and only goes out of the way when Jack Birch shows his sallow face: for she can't bear him, and always finds work when he comes near.

How different she is when some folks approach her! I won't be presumptuous; but I think, I think, I have made a not unfavourable impression in some quarters. However, let us be mum on this subject. I like to see her, because she always looks good-humoured; because she is always kind, because she is always modest, because she is fond of those poor little brats—orphans some of them,—because she is rather pretty, I dare say, or because I think so, which comes to the same thing.

Though she is kind to all, it must be owned she shows the most gross favouritism towards the amiable children. She brings them cakes from dessert, and regales them with Zoe's preserves; spends many of her little shillings in presents for her favourites, and will tell them stories by the hour. She has one very sad story about a little boy, who died long ago; the younger children are never weary of hearing about him; and Miss Raby has shown to one of them a lock of the little chap's hair, which she keeps in her work-box to this day.

THE DEAR BROTHERS

A Melodrama in several Rounds.

The Doctor.

Mr. Tipper, Uncle to the Masters Boxall.

Boxall Major, Boxall Minor, Brown, Jones, Smith,

Robinson, Tiffin Minimus.

B. Go it old Boxall.

J. Give it him young Boxall.

R. Pitch into him old Boxall.

S. Two to one on young Boxall.

[Enter Tiffin Minimus, running.

Tiffin Minimus. Boxalls! you 're wanted.

(The Doctor to Mr. Tipper.) Every boy in the school loves them, my dear sir; your nephews are a credit to my establishment. They are orderly, well-conducted, gentleman-like boys. Let us enter and find them at their studies.

[Enter The Doctor and Mr. Tipper.

GRAND TABLEAU.

A HOPELESS CASE

Let us, people who are so uncommonly clever and learned, have a great tenderness and pity for the poor folks who are not endowed with the prodigious talents which we have. I have always had a regard for dunces;—those of my own school-days were amongst the pleasantest of the fellows, and have turned out by no means the dullest in life; whereas many a youth who could turn off Latin hexameters by the yard, and construe Greek quite glibly, is no better than a feeble prig now, with not a pennyworth more brains than were in his head before his beard grew.

Those poor dunces! Talk of being the last man, ah! what a pang it must be to be the last boy—huge, misshapen, fourteen years of age,—and "taken up" by a chap who is but six years old, and can't speak quite plain yet!

Master Hulker is in that condition at Birch's. He is the most honest, kind, active, plucky, generous creature. He can do many things better than most boys. He can go up a tree, jump, play at cricket, dive and swim perfectly—he can eat twice as much as almost any lady (as Miss Birch well knows), he has a pretty talent at carving figures with his hack-knife, he makes and paints little coaches, he can take a watch to pieces and put it together again. He can do everything but learn his lesson; and there he sticks at the bottom of the school, hopeless. As the little boys are drafted in from Miss Raby's class, (it is true she is one of the best instructresses in the world,) they enter and hop over poor Hulker. He would be handed over to the governess only he is too big. Sometimes I used to think, that this desperate stupidity was a stratagem of the poor rascal's; and that he shammed dulness so that he might be degraded into

Miss Raby's class: if she would teach me, I know, before George, I would put on a pinafore and a little jacket—but no, it is a natural incapacity for the Latin Grammar.

If you could see his grammar, it is a perfect curiosity of dog's ears. The leaves and cover are all curled and ragged. Many of the pages are worn away, with the rubbing of his elbows as he sits poring over the hopeless volume, with the blows of his fists as he thumps it madly, or with the poor fellow's tears. You see him wiping them away with the back of his hand, as he tries and tries, and can't do it.

When I think of that Latin Grammar, and that infernal As in Præsenti, and of other things which I was made to learn in my youth: upon my conscience I am surprised that we ever survived it. When one thinks of the boys who have been caned because they could not master that intolerable jargon! Good Lord, what a pitiful chorus these poor little creatures send up! Be gentle with them, ye schoolmasters, and only whop those who won't learn.

The Doctor has operated upon Hulker (between ourselves), but the boy was so little affected you would have thought he had taken chloroform. Birch is weary of whipping now, and leaves the boy to go his own gait. Prince, when he hears the lesson, and who cannot help making fun of a fool, adopts the sarcastic manner with Master Hulker, and says, "Mr. Hulker, may I take the liberty to inquire if your brilliant intellect has enabled you to perceive the difference between those words which grammarians have defined as substantive and adjective nouns?—if not, perhaps Mr. Ferdinand Timmins will instruct you." And Timmins hops over Hulker's head.

I wish Prince would leave off girding at the poor lad. He's an only son, and his mother is a widow woman, who loves him with all her might. There is a famous sneer about the suckling of fools and the chronicling of small beer; but remember it was a rascal who uttered it.

A WORD ABOUT MISS BIRCH

"The Gentlemen, and especially the younger and more tender of the Pupils, will have the advantage of the constant superintendence and affectionate care of Miss Zoe Birch, sister of the Principal: whose dearest aim will be to supply (as far as may be) the absent maternal friend."—Prospectus of Rodwell Regis School.

This is all very fine in the Doctor's circulars, and Miss Zoe Birch—(a sweet birch blossom it is, fifty-five years old, during two score of which she has dosed herself with pills; with a nose as red and a face as sour as a crab-apple)—may do mighty well in a prospectus. But I should like to know who would take Miss Zoe for a mother, or would have her for one?

The only persons in the house who are not afraid of her are Miss Flora and I—no, I am afraid of her, though I do know the story about the French usher in 1830—but all the rest tremble before the woman, from the Doctor down to poor Francis the knife-boy, and whom she bullies into his miserable blacking-hole.

The Doctor is a pompous and outwardly severe man—but inwardly weak and easy: loving a joke and a glass of port wine. I get on with him, therefore, much better than Mr. Prince, who scorns him for an ass, and under whose keen eyes the worthy Doctor writhes like a convicted impostor; and many a sunshiny afternoon would he have said, "Mr. T., Sir, shall we try another glass of that yellow sealed wine which you seem to like?" (and which he likes even better than I do), had not the old harridan of a Zoe been down upon us, and insisted on turning me out with her miserable weak coffee. She a mother indeed! A sour milk generation she would have nursed. She is always croaking, scolding, bullying,—yowling at the housemaids, snarling at Miss Raby, bowwowing after the little boys, barking after the big ones. She knows how much every boy eats to an ounce; and her delight is to ply with fat the little ones who can't bear it, and with raw meat those who hate underdone. It was she who caused the Doctor to be eaten out three times; and nearly created a rebellion in the school because she insisted on his flogging Goliah Longman.

The only time that woman is happy is when she comes in of a morning to the little boys' dormitories with a cup of hot Epsom salts, and a sippet of bread. Boo!—the very notion makes me quiver. She stands over them. I saw her do it to young Byles only a few days since—and her presence makes the abomination doubly abominable.

As for attending them in real illness, do you suppose that she would watch a single night for any one of them? Not she. When poor little Charley Davison (that child, a lock of whose soft hair I have said how Miss Raby still keeps) lay ill of scarlet fever in the holidays—for the Colonel, the father of these boys, was in India—it was Anne Raby who tended the child, who watched him all through the fever, who never left him while it lasted, or until she had closed the little eyes that were never to brighten or moisten more. Anny watched and deplored him, but it was Miss Birch who wrote the letter announcing his demise, and got the gold chain and locket which the Colonel ordered as a memento of his gratitude. It was through a row with Miss Birch that Frank Davison ran away. I promise you that after he joined his regiment in India, the Ahmednuggar Irregulars, which his gallant father commands, there came over no more annual shawls and presents to Dr. and Miss Birch, and that if she fancied the Colonel was coming home to marry her (on account of her tenderness to his motherless children, which he was always writing about), that notion was very soon given up. But these affairs are of early date, seven years back, and I only heard of them in a very confused manner from Miss Raby, who was a girl, and had just come to Rodwell Regis. She is always very much moved when she speaks about those boys, which is but seldom. I take it the death of the little one still grieves her tender heart.

Yes, it is Miss Birch, who has turned away seventeen ushers and second masters in eleven years, and half as many French masters; inconsolable, I suppose, since the departure of her favourite, M. Grinche, with her gold watch, &c.; but this is only surmise—and what I gather from the taunts of Miss Rosa when she and her aunt have a tiff at tea.

But besides this, I have another way of keeping her in order.

Whenever she is particularly odious or insolent to Miss Raby, I have but to introduce raspberry jam into the conversation, and the woman holds her tongue. She will understand me. I need not say more.

Note, 12th December.—I may speak now. I have left the place and don't mind. I say then at once, and without caring twopence for the consequences, that I saw this woman, this mother of the boys, eating jam with a spoon out of Master Wiggins's trunk in the box-room; and of this I am ready to take an affidavit any day.

THIS DRAMA OUGHT TO BE REPRESENTED IN ABOUT SIX CUTS.

[The School is hushed. Lawrence the Prefect, and Custos of the rods, is marching after the Doctor into the operating-room. Master Backhouse is about to follow.]

Master Backhouse. It's all very well, but you see if I don't pay you out after school—you sneak, you.

Master Lurcher. If you do I '1l tell again.

[Exit Backhouse.

[The rod is heard from the adjoining apartment.
Hwish—Hhwish—hwish—hwish—hwish—hwish—hwish.]

[Re-enter Backhouse.

BRIGGS IN LUCK

Enter the Knife-boy.—Hamper for Briggses!

Master Brown.—Hurray, Tom Briggs! I'll lend you my knife.

If this story does not carry its own moral, what fable does, I wonder? Before the arrival of that hamper, Master Briggs was in no better repute than any other young gentleman of the lower school; and in fact I had occasion myself, only lately, to correct Master Brown for kicking his friend's shins during the writing-lesson. But how this basket directed by his mother's housekeeper, and marked "Glass with care," (whence I conclude that it contains some jam and some bottles of wine probably, as well as the usual cake and game-pie, and half a sovereign for the elder Master B., and five new shillings for Master Decimus Briggs)—how, I say, the arrival of this basket, alters all Master Briggs's circumstances in life, and the estimation in which many persons regard him!

If he is a good-hearted boy, as I have reason to think, the very first thing he will do, before inspecting the contents of the hamper, or cutting into them with the knife which Master Brown has so considerately lent him; will be to read over the letter from home which lies on the top of the parcel. He does so, as I remark to Miss Raby (for whom I happened to be mending pens when the little circumstance arose), with a flushed face and winking eyes. Look how the other boys are peering into the basket as he reads.—I say to her, "Isn't it a pretty picture?" Part of the letter is in a very large hand. That is from his little sister. And I would wager that she netted the little purse which he has just taken out of it, and which Master Lynx is eyeing.

"You are a droll man, and remark all sorts of queer things," Miss Raby says, smiling, and plying her swift needle and fingers as quick as possible.

"I am glad we are both on the spot, and that the little fellow lies under our guns as it were, and so is protected from some such brutal school-pirates as young Duval for instance, who would rob him probably of some of those good things, good in themselves, and better because fresh from home. See, there is a pie as I said, and which I dare say is better than those which are served at our table (but you never take any notice of these kind of things, Miss Raby), a cake of course, a bottle of currant wine, jam-pots, and no end of pears in the straw.

"With this money little Briggs will be able to pay the tick which that imprudent child has run up with Mrs. Ruggles; and I shall let Briggs Major pay for the pencil-case which Bullock sold to him.—It will be a lesson to the young prodigal for the future.

"But, I say, what a change there will be in his life for some time to come, and at least until his present wealth is spent! The boys who bully him will mollify towards him, and accept his pie and sweetmeats. They will have feasts in the bed-room; and that wine will taste more deliciously to them than the best out of the Doctor's cellar. The cronies will be invited. Young Master Wagg will tell his most dreadful story and sing his best song for a slice of that pie. What a jolly night they will have! When we go the rounds at night, Mr. Prince and I will take care to make a noise before we come to Briggs's room, so that the boys may have time to put the light out, to push the things away, and to scud into bed. Doctor Spry may be put in requisition the next morning..."

"Nonsense! you absurd creature," cries out Miss Raby, laughing; and I lay down the twelfth pen very nicely mended.

"Yes; after luxury comes the doctor, I say; after extravagance, a hole in the breeches pocket. To judge from his disposition, Briggs Major will not be much better off a couple of days hence than he is now, and, if I am not mistaken, will end life a poor man. Brown will be kicking his shins before a week is over, depend upon it. There are boys and men of all sorts, Miss R.—there are selfish sneaks who hoard until the store they daren't use grows mouldy—there are spendthrifts who fling away, parasites who flatter and lick its shoes, and snarling curs who hate and envy, good fortune."—I put down the last of the pens, brushing away with it the quill-chips from her desk first, and she looked at me with a kind wondering face. I brushed them away, clicked the pen-knife into my pocket, made her a bow, and walked off—for the bell was ringing for school.

A YOUNG FELLOW WHO IS PRETTY SURE TO SUCCEED

If Master Briggs is destined in all probability to be a poor man, the chances are, that Mr. Bullock will have a very different lot. He is a son of a partner of the eminent banking firm of Bullock and Hulker, Lombard Street, and very high in the upper school—quite out of my jurisdiction, consequently.

He writes the most beautiful current hand ever seen; and the way in which he mastered arithmetic (going away into recondite and wonderful rules in the Tutor's Assistant, which some masters even dare not approach) is described by the Doctor in terms of admiration. He is Mr. Prince's best algebra pupil; and a very fair classic, too, doing everything well for which he has a mind.

He does not busy himself with the sports of his comrades, and holds a cricket-bat no better than Miss Raby would. He employs the play hours in improving his mind, and reading the newspaper; he is a profound politician, and, it must be owned, on the Liberal side. The elder boys despise him rather; and when Champion Major passes, he turns his head, and looks down. I don't like the expression of Bullock's narrow, green eyes, as they follow the elder Champion, who does not seem to know or care how much the other hates him.

No—Mr. Bullock, though perhaps the cleverest and most accomplished boy in the school, associates with the quite little boys when he is minded for society. To these he is quite affable, courteous, and winning. He never fagged or thrashed one them. He has done the verses and corrected the exercises of many, and many is the little lad to whom he has lent a little money.

It is true he charges at the rate of a penny a week for every sixpence lent out, but many a fellow to whom tarts are a present necessity is happy to pay this interest for the loan. These transactions are kept secret. Mr. Bullock, in rather a whining tone, when he takes Master Green aside and does the requisite business for him, says, "You know you'll go and talk about it everywhere. I don't want to lend you the money, I want to buy something with it. It's only to oblige you; and yet I am sure you will go and make fun of me." Whereon, of course, Green, eager for the money, vows solemnly that the transaction shall be confidential, and only speaks when the payment of the interest becomes oppressive.

Thus it is that Mr. Bullock's practices are at all known. At a very early period indeed his commercial genius manifested itself; and by happy speculations in toffey; by composing a sweet drink made of stick liquorice and brown sugar, and selling it at a profit to the younger children; by purchasing a series of novels, which he let out at an adequate remuneration; by doing boys exercises for a penny, and other processes, he showed the bent of his mind. At the end of the half year he always went home richer than when he arrived at school, with his purse full of money.

Nobody knows how much he brought: but the accounts are fabulous. Twenty, thirty, fifty—it is impossible to say how many sovereigns. When joked about his money, he turns pale and swears he has not a shilling: whereas he has had a banker's account ever since he was thirteen years old.

At the present moment he is employed in negotiating the sale of a knife with Master Green, and is pointing out to the latter the beauty of the six blades, and that he need not pay until after the holidays.

Champion Major has sworn that he will break every bone in his skin the next time that he cheats a little boy, and is bearing down upon him. Let us come away. It is frightful to see that big peaceful clever coward moaning under well deserved blows and whining for mercy.

DUVAL, THE PIRATE

(Jones Minimus passes, laden with tarts.)

Duval. Hullo! you small boy with the tarts! Come here, Sir.

Jones Minimus. Please, Duval, they ain't mine.

Duval. O you abominable young story-teller.

[He confiscates the goods.

I think I like young Duval's mode of levying contributions better than Bullock's. The former's, at least, has the merit of more candour. Duval is the pirate of Birch's, and lies in wait for small boys laden with money or provender. He scents plunder from afar off: and pounces out on it. Woe betide the little fellow when Duval boards him!

There was a youth here whose money I used to keep, as he was of an extravagant and weak disposition; and I doled it out to him in weekly shillings, sufficient for the purchase of the necessary tarts. This boy came to me one day for half a sovereign, for a very particular purpose, he said. I afterwards found he wanted to lend the money to Duval.

The young ogre burst out laughing, when in a great wrath and fury I ordered him to refund to the little boy: and proposed a bill of exchange at three months. It is true Duval's father does not pay the Doctor, and the lad never has a shilling, save that which he levies; and though he is always bragging about the splendour of Freenystown, Co. Cork, and the fox-hounds his father keeps, and the claret they drink there—there comes no remittance from Castle Freeny in these bad times to the honest Doctor, who is a kindly man enough, and never yet turned an insolvent boy out of doors.

THE DORMITORIES

MASTER HEWLETT AND MASTER NIGHTINGALE.

(Rather a cold winter night.)

Hewlett (flinging a shoe at Master Nightingale's bed, with which he hits that young gentleman.) Hullo! You! Get up and bring me that shoe.

Nightingale. Yes, Hewlett. (He gets up.)

Hewlett. Don't drop it, and be very careful of it, Sir.

Nightingale. Yes, Hewlett.

Hewlett. Silence in the Dormitory! Any boy who opens his mouth I'll murder him. Now, Sir, are not you the boy what can sing?

Nightingale. Yes, Hewlett.

Hewlett. Chaunt then till I go to sleep, and if I wake when you stop, you 'll have this at your head.

[Master Hewlett lays his Bluchers on the bed, ready to shy at Master Nightingale's head in the case contemplated.

Nightingale (timidly.) Please, Hewlett?

Hewlett. Well, Sir.

Nightingale. May I put on my trowsers, please? Hewlett. No, Sir. Go on, or I '11—

Nightingale,

"Through pleasures and palaces

Though we may roam,

Be it ever so humble,

There's no place like home.

"Home, home! sweet, sweet home!

There's no place like ho-ome!

There's no place like home!"

(Da Capo.)

A CAPTURE AND A RESCUE

My young friend, Patrick Champion, George's younger brother, is a late arrival among us; has much of the family quality and good-nature; is not in the least a tyrant to the small boys, but is as eager as an Amadis to fight. He is boxing his way up the school, emulating his great brother. He fixes his eye on a boy above him in strength or size, and you hear somehow that a difference has arisen between them at football, and they have their coats off presently. He has thrashed himself over the heads of many youths in this manner; for instance, if Champion can lick Dobson, who can thrash Hobson, how much more, then, can he thrash Hobson. Thus he works up and establishes his position in the school. Nor does Mr. Prince think it advisable that we ushers should walk much in the way when these little differences are being settled, unless there is some gross disparity, or danger is apprehended.

For instance, I own to having seen the row depicted here as I was shaving at my bed-room window. I did not hasten down to prevent its consequences. Fogle had confiscated a top, the property of Snivins, the which, as the little wretch was always pegging it at my toes, I did not regret. Snivins whimpered; and young Champion came up, lusting for battle. Directly he made out Fogle, he steered for him, pulling up his coat-sleeves, and clearing for action.

"Who spoke to you, young Champion?" Fogle said, and he flung down the top to Master Snivins. I knew there would be no fight; and perhaps Champion, too, was disappointed.

THE GARDEN, WHERE THE PARLOUR-BOARDERS GO

Noblemen have been rather scarce at Birch's—but the heir of a great Prince has been living with the Doctor for some years.—He is Lord George Gaunt's eldest son, the noble Plan-tagenet Gaunt Gaunt, and nephew of the Most Honourable the Marquis of Steyne.

They are very proud of him at the Doctor's—and the two Misses and Papa, whenever a stranger comes down whom they want to dazzle, are pretty sure to bring Lord Steyne into the conversation, mentioning the last party at Gaunt House, and cursorily remarking that they have with them a young friend who will be in all human probability Marquis of Steyne and Earl of Gaunt, &c.

Plantagenet does not care much about these future honours: provided he can get some brown sugar on his bread and butter, or sit with three chairs and play at coach and horses, quite quietly by himself, he is tolerably happy. He saunters in and out of school when he likes, and looks at the masters and other boys with a listless grin. He used to be taken to church, but he laughed and talked in odd places, so they are forced to leave him at home now. He will sit with a bit of string and play cats-cradle for many hours. He likes to go and join the very small children at their games. Some are frightened at him, but they soon cease to fear, and order him about. I have seen him go and fetch tarts from Mrs. Ruggles for a boy of eight years old; and cry bitterly if he did not get a piece. He cannot speak quite plain, but very nearly; and is not more, I suppose, than three-and-twenty.

Of course at home they know his age, though they never come and see him. But they forget that Miss Rosa Birch is no longer a young chit as she was ten years ago, when Gaunt was brought to the school. On the contrary, she has had no small experience in the tender passion, and is at this moment smitten with a disinterested affection for Plantagenet Gaunt.

Next to a little doll with a burnt nose, which he hides away in cunning places, Mr. Gaunt is very fond of Miss Rosa too. What a pretty match it would make! and how pleased they would be at Gaunt House, if the grandson and heir of the great Marquis of Steyne, the descendant of a hundred Gaunts and Tudors, should marry Miss Birch, the schoolmaster's daughter! It is true she has the sense on her side, and poor Plantagenet is only an idiot: but there he is, a zany, with such expectations and such a pedigree!

If Miss Rosa would run away with Mr. Gaunt, she would leave off bullying her cousin, Miss Anny Raby. Shall I put her up to the notion, and offer to lend her the money to run away? Mr. Gaunt is not allowed money. He had some once, but Bullock took him into a corner, and got it from him. He has a moderate tick opened at the tart-woman's. He stops at Rodwell Regis through the year, school-time and holiday time; it is all the same to him. Nobody asks about him, or thinks about him, save twice a year, when the Doctor goes to Gaunt House, and gets the amount of his bills, and a glass of wine in the steward's room.

And yet you see somehow that he is a gentleman. His manner is different to that of the owners of that coarse table and parlour at which he is a boarder, (I do not speak of Miss R. of course, for her manners are as good as those of a Duchess). When he caught Miss Rosa boxing little Fiddes's ears, his face grew red, and he broke into a fierce, inarticulate rage. After that, and for some days, he used to shrink from her; but they are reconciled now. I saw them this afternoon in the garden, where only the parlour-boarders walk. He was playful, and touched her with his stick. She raised her handsome eyes in surprise, and smiled on him very kindly.

The thing was so clear, that I thought it my duty to speak to old Zoe about it. The wicked old catamaran told me she wished that some people would mind their own business, and hold their tongues—that some people were paid to teach writing, and not to tell tales and make mischief: and I have since been thinking whether I ought to communicate with the Doctor.

THE OLD PUPIL

As I came into the play-grounds this morning, I saw a dashing young fellow, with a tanned face and a blonde moustache, who was walking up and down the green, arm-in-arm with Champion Major, and followed by a little crowd of boys.

They were talking of old times evidently. "What had become of Irvine and Smith?"—"Where was Bill Harris and Jones, not Squinny Jones, but Cocky Jones?"—and so forth. The gentleman was no stranger; he was an old pupil evidently, come to see if any of his old comrades remained, and to revisit the cari luogi of his youth.

Champion was evidently proud of his arm-fellow. He espied his brother, young Champion, and introduced him. "Come here, Sir," he called. "The young 'un wasn't here in your time, Davison."

"Pat, Sir," said he, "this is Captain Davison, one of Birch's boys. Ask him who was among the first in the lines at Sobraon?"

Pat's face kindled up as he looked Davison full in the face, and held out his hand. Old Champion and Davison both blushed. The infantry set up a "Hurray! hurray! hurray!" Champion leading, and waving his wide-awake. I protest that the scene did one good to witness. Here was the hero and cock of the school come back to see his old haunts and cronies. He had always remembered them. Since he had seen them last, he had faced death and achieved honour. But for my dignity I would have shied up my hat too.

With a resolute step, and his arm still linked in Champion's, Captain Davison now advanced, followed by a wake of little boys, to that corner of the green where Mrs. Buggies has her tart-stand.

"Hullo, Mother Buggies! don't you remember me?" he said, and shook her by the hand.

"Lor, if it ain't Davison Major!" she said. "Well, Davison Major, you owe me fourpence for two sausage-rolls from when you went away."

Davison laughed, and all the little crew of boys set up a similar chorus.

"I buy the whole shop," he said. "Now, young 'uns—eat away!"

Then there was such a "Hurray! hurray!" as surpassed the former cheer in loudness. Everybody engaged in it except Piggy Duff, who made an instant dash at the three-cornered puffs, but was stopped by Champion, who said there should be a fair distribution. And so there was, and no one lacked, neither of raspberry open-tarts, nor of mellifluous bull's-eyes, nor of polonies, beautiful to the sight and taste.

The hurraying brought out the Doctor himself, who put his hand up to his spectacles and started when he saw the old pupil. Each blushed when he recognised the other; for seven years ago they had parted not good friends.

"What—Davison?" the Doctor said, with a tremulous voice. "God bless you, my dear fellow!"—and they shook hands. "A half-holiday, of course, boys," he added, and there was another hurray: there was to be no end to the cheering that day.

"How's—how's the family, Sir?" Captain Davison asked.

"Come in and see. Flora's grown quite a lady. Dine with us, of course. Champion Major, come to dinner at five. Mr. Titmarsh, the pleasure of your company?" The Doctor swung open the garden-gate: the old master and pupil entered the house reconciled.

I thought I would just peep into Miss Raby's room, and tell her of this event. She was working away at her linen there, as usual, quiet and cheerful.

"You should put up," I said with a smile; "the Doctor has given us a half-holiday."

"I never have holidays," Miss Raby replied.

Then I told her of the scene I had just witnessed, of the arrival of the old pupil, the purchase of the tarts, the proclamation of the holiday, and the shouts of the boys of "Hurray, Davison."

"Who is it?" cried out Miss Raby, starting and turning as white as a sheet.

I told her it was Captain Davison from India, and described the appearance and behaviour of the Captain. When I had finished speaking, she asked me to go and get her a glass of water; she felt unwell. But she was gone when I came back with the water.

I know all now. After sitting for a quarter of an hour with the Doctor, who attributed his guest's uneasiness no doubt to his desire to see Miss Laura Birch, Davison started up and said he wanted to see Miss Raby. "You remember, Sir, how kind she was to my little brother," he said. Whereupon the Doctor, with a look of surprise that anybody should want to see Miss Raby, said she was in the little school-room, whither the Captain went, knowing the way from old times.

A few minutes afterwards, Miss B. and Miss Z. returned from a drive with Plantagenet Gaunt in their one-horse fly, and being informed of Davison's arrival, and that he was closeted with Miss Raby in the little school-room, of course made for that apartment at once. I was coming into it from the other door. I wanted to know whether she had drunk the water.

This is what both parties saw. The two were in this very attitude. "Well, upon my word!" cries out Miss Zoe, But Davison did not let go his hold; and Miss Raby's head only sank down on his hand.

"You must get another governess, Sir, for the little boys," Frank Davison said to the Doctor. "Anny Raby has promised to come with me."

You may suppose I shut to the door on my side. And when I returned to the little school-room, it was blank and empty. Everybody was gone. I could hear the boys shouting at play in the green, outside. The glass of water was on the table where I had placed it. I took it and drank it myself, to the health of Anny Raby and her husband. It was rather a choker.

But of course I wasn't going to stop on at Birch's. When his young friends re-assemble on the 1st of February next, they will have two new masters. Prince resigned too, and is at present living with me at my old lodgings at Mrs. Cammysole's. If any nobleman or gentleman wants a private tutor for his son, a note to the Rev. F. Prince will find him there.

Miss Clapperclaw says we are both a couple of old fools; and that she knew, when I set off last year to Rodwell Regis, after meeting the two young ladies at a party at General Champion's house in our street, that I was going on a goose's errand. Well, well, that journey is over now; I shall dine at the General's on Christmas-day, where I shall meet Captain and Mrs. Davison, and some of the old pupils of Birch's; and I wish a merry Christmas to them, and to all young and old boys.

|The play is done; the curtain drops,
Slow falling, to the prompter's bell:
A moment yet the actor stops,

And looks around, to say farewell.
It is an irksome word and task;
And when he 's laughed and said his say,
He shows, as he removes the mask,
A face that's anything but gay.

One word, ere yet the evening ends,
Let's close it with a parting rhyme,
And pledge a hand to all young friends,
As fits the merry Christmas-time.
On life's wide scene you, too, have parts,
That Fate ere long shall bid you play;
Good night! with honest gentle hearts
A kindly greeting go alway!

Good night!—I'd say, the griefs, the joys,
Just hinted in this mimic page,
The triumphs and defeats of boys,
Are but repeated in our age.
I 'd say, your woes were not less keen,
Your hopes more vain, than those of men;
Your pangs or pleasures of fifteen,
At forty-five played o'er again.

I'd say, we suffer and we strive
Not less nor more as men than boys;
With grizzled beards at forty-five,
As erst at twelve, in corduroys.
And if, in time of sacred youth,
We learned at home to love and pray,
Pray Heaven, that early Love and Truth
May never wholly pass away.

And in the world, as in the school,
I 'd say, how fate may change and shift;
The prize be sometimes with the fool,
The race not always to the swift.
The strong may yield, the good may fall,
The great man he a vulgar clown,
The knave be lifted over all,
The kind cast pitilessly down.

Who knows the inscrutable design?
Blessed be He who took and gave!
Why should your mother, Charles, not mine,
Be weeping at her darling's grave? *
We bow to Heaven that will'd it so,
That darkly rules the fate of all,
That sends the respite or the blow,
That's free to give or to recall.
This crowns his feast with wine and wit:
Who brought him to that mirth aud state?
His betters, see, below him sit,
Or hunger hopeless at the gate.
Who bade the mud from Dives' wheel
To spurn the rags of Lazarus?
Come, brother, in that dust we '11 kneel,
Confessing Heaven that ruled it thus.

C. B., ob. 29 Nov. 1848, set. 42.

So each shall mourn, in life's advance,
Dear hopes, dear friends, untimely killed;
Shall grieve for many a forfeit chance,
And longing passion unfulfilled.
Amen! whatever fate be sent,—
Pray God the heart may kindly glow,
Although the heart with cares be bent,
And whitened with the winter-snow.

Come wealth or want, come good or ill,
Let young and old accept their part,
And bow before the Awful Will,
And bear it with an honest heart.
Who misses, or who wins the prize?
Go, lose or conquer as you can:
But if you fail, or if you rise,
Be each, pray God, a gentleman,

A gentleman, or old or young!

(Bear kindly with my humble lays);
The sacred chorus first was sung
Upon the first of Christmas-days:
The shepherds heard it overhead—
The joyful angels raised it then:
Glory to Heaven on high, it said,
And peace on earth to gentle men.

My song, save this, is little worth;
I lay the weary pen aside,
And wish you health, and love, and mirth,
As fits the solemn Christmas-tide.
As fits the holy Christmas birth,
Be this, good friends, our carol still—
Be peace on earth, be peace on earth,
To men of gentle will.

William Makepeace Thackeray – A Short Biography

William Makepeace Thackeray, was born on July 18th, 1811 in Calcutta, then British India, where his father, Richmond Thackeray was the secretary to the Board of Revenue in the British East India Company. His mother, Anne Becher also worked for the British East India Company.

His father died in 1815, and his mother sent Thackeray to England the following year while she remained in India and would, sometime later, marry her childhood sweetheart. En-route to England the ship stopped for provisions on St. Helena. The Imprisoned Napoleon was pointed out to him by a servant with the words that he "eats three sheep every day, and all the little children he can lay hands on!"

Finally, back in England the young Thackeray was sent to school, initially in Southampton and Chiswick, before being moved to Charterhouse School. Charterhouse and Thackeray did not take to each other but the time became a valuable source for his later work "Slaughterhouse". Despite his less than respectful recalling of his time with them Charterhouse placed a monument in the chapel after his death.

In his final year at Charterhouse a troubling illness delayed his departure to attend Cambridge University. Over the course of his life Thackeray would suffer from ill health, much of it brought about for his fondness for "gluttling and gorging". Excess was something he could enjoy and for a man who stood some 6' 3" it would appear to the eye that, initially at least, his large frame could absorb much of that excess.

However, Thackeray's lazy attitude to completely mastering anything he set his mind too, especially where ambition for academia was involved, meant he departed Cambridge little more than a year after joining. He had however published two short works in University periodicals. As an author, he would have quite some impact on English literature in the years to come, so it seems difficult to reconcile that he felt no urgency to pursue writing at that time.

He now spent some time travelling across Europe stopping at both Paris, to study art, and to winter in Weimar. Back in London a final attempt was made on a professional career. This time studying law at Middle Temple. It lasted no more than a few months.

Now, having reached 21, he received his father's inheritance. It was a very substantial estate of 17,000 pounds, an enormous sum of money at the time. However, although Thackeray had youth he lacked a little in energy and certainly much financial experience. He funded not one but two newspapers, and neither was to prove successful. Gambling seemed enjoyable and certainly he had money to lose, which he did on a regular basis. Further investments in two soon-to-fail Indian banks quickly ensured little of his good fortune remained.

He now had to consider taking up yet another profession. Thackeray turned to art hoping that his studies in Paris would prove of benefit. Unfortunately, they did not. His ambivalent attitude continued until on August 20th, 1836 he married the 20-year-old, Isabella Gethin Shawe. It seemed to prove a turning point in many ways.

The marriage would produce three daughters; Anne Isabella in 1837, Jane, in 1838, who tragically died in infancy and Harriet Marian in 1840.

Now, as a husband and father, Thackeray seemed at last to understand his responsibilities to nurture and provide.

His early efforts at "writing for his life" were to establish his career as a foremost author. His main employment was with Fraser's Magazine, a sharp-witted and sharp-tongued conservative publication for which he produced art criticism, short fictional sketches, and who would also serialise two of his novels. He also found time, between 1837 and 1840 to review books for The Times and to make regular contributions to The Morning Chronicle and The Foreign Quarterly Review.

In his earliest works, which he wrote under various pseudonyms including; Charles James Yellowplush, Michael Angelo Titmarsh and George Savage Fitz-Boodle, he tended towards savagery in his attacks on high society, military prowess, the institution of marriage and hypocrisy.

Between May 1839 and February 1840 Fraser's published Catherine. Originally intended as a satire of the Newgate school of crime fiction, it ended up being more of a picaresque tale. Thackeray also began work on what would eventually become A Shabby Genteel Story.

However, Thackeray, having successfully found a career that he cared about and had the talent for, found that his personal life was about to descend into chaos. After the birth of her third child in 1840, Isabella, sank into depression. At first Thackeray, didn't think too much of it. He needed to work to earn an income to support his family and finding that Isabella was distracting both herself and him he realised he could get no work done at home and so spent more and more time away until finally, in September 1840, it dawned upon him how serious his wife's condition had become. Struck by guilt, he set out with his wife to Ireland. During the boat crossing she threw herself into the sea, but was thankfully pulled from the waters. Her mother who had little understanding of her daughter's illness was of little help and perhaps a hinderance. After four-weeks they returned to England. From November 1840 to February 1842 Isabella was in and out of professional care, as her condition waxed and waned.

Isabella eventually deteriorated into a permanent state of detachment. Thackeray desperately sought cures for her, but nothing worked, and she ended up in two different asylums in or near Paris until 1845, after which Thackeray took her back to England, where he installed her with a Mrs Bakewell at Camberwell. Despite her condition Isabella would outlive her husband by 3 decades.

After his wife's illness Thackeray became a de facto widower, never able to establish another permanent relationship.

In 1843, through his connection to the illustrator John Leech, whom he had met at Charterhouse, he began writing for the newly created magazine Punch, in which he published The Snob Papers, later collected as The Book of Snobs. Thackeray was a regular contributor to Punch until 1854.

Thackeray had earlier received some success with two travel books, The Paris Sketch Book and The Irish Sketch Book, the latter marked by hostility to Irish Catholics. The book appealed to British prejudices, and on that basis Thackeray now became Punch's Irish expert, often under the pseudonym Hibernis Hibernior. It was Thackeray's writings that were the basis for Punch's notoriously harsh, hostile and condescending depictions of the Irish during the devastating Irish Famine (1845–51).

As well as his regular columns and contributions Thackeray worked on his novels. In The Luck of Barry Lyndon, which was serialised in Fraser's in 1844, he explored the situation of an outsider trying to achieve status in high society, a theme he developed more successfully a few years later with Vanity Fair.

Thackeray achieved more recognition with his Snob Papers (serialised 1846/7, and published as a book in 1848), but the work that really established his fame was the novel Vanity Fair, which first appeared in serialised instalments beginning in January 1847.

Published as a book the novel had a slow start but eventually sales rose to 7,000 copies a month. Just as importantly, it was the book that everybody was talking about. Thackeray finally had a name that gained notice and was reviewed in journals such as the famed, and much sought after, Edinburgh Review.

The accolades and success also gave him a respite from writing everything in a manner that would help ensure income rather than literary respect. Even before Vanity Fair completed its serial run Thackeray had become a celebrity, sought after by the very lords and ladies whom he satirised. with the character of Becky Sharp, the artist's daughter who rises high by manipulating all around her.

Pendennis followed in 1849-50, but it was interrupted halfway through writing for 3 months by a severe illness. Some accounts say it was cholera. Pendennis is a semi-autobiographical bildungsroman that draws on, among other things, Thackeray's disappointments in college, his ambivalent relationship with his mother, and his insider's knowledge of the London publishing world.

This novel ran at the same time as Charles Dicken's David Copperfield, and their dual appearance brought about the first of many comparisons with Dickens. Thackeray, for his part, felt that he and Dickens were battling for supremacy, though he would never equal Dickens's popularity, except with the critics.

Interestingly the two were involved in a spat which became known as the "Garrick Club affair". Thackeray and Dickens had skirmished over the "Dignity of Literature" and had other slight disagreements but this literary quarrel caused a rift in their friendship that lasted almost until the end of Thackeray's life. The relationship was healed only in Thackeray's last months, through a surprise meeting and handshake on the steps of a London club. Thackeray had taken offense at some personal remarks in a column by Edmund Yates and demanded an apology, eventually taking the affair to the Garrick Club committee. Already upset with Thackeray for an indiscreet remark about his affair with Ellen Ternan, Dickens championed Yates, helping him to write letters both to Thackeray and, in his defense, to the club's committee. Despite the intervention of Dickens, Yates eventually lost the vote of the Club's members, but the quarrel was laid out for the public in journal articles and pamphlets. "What pains me most," Thackeray said at the time, "is that Dickens should have been his adviser, and next that I should have had to lay a heavy hand on a young man who, I take it, has been cruelly punished by the issue of the affair, and I believe is hardly aware of the nature of his own offence, and doesn't even now understand that a gentleman should resent the monstrous insult which he volunteered".

Aside from these quarrelsome, distracting literary disagreements and Isabella's on-going illness life was good for Thackeray. He was to remain as he put it "at the top of the tree," for the rest of his life. The works for which he is so well remembered; Vanity Fair and Barry Lyndon had established that but he continued to write and produce novels, stories, sketches and works profusely.

To remain at such a high level in both quality and quantity is somewhat surprising given the continuation and escalation of various illnesses which continued to haunt him.

With Isabella still unwell Thackeray did seek out other women, in particular Mrs Jane Brookfield. Despite his hopes, it always felt that he was pursuing her as she battled the problems of her own marriage and turned to Thackeray for comfort and support. A source for these relationships often came on the lecture tours of Great Britain and the United States which he now entertained. These tours gave the public a chance to see and hear their hero's and provided another valuable source of income for those invited to tour. Whilst in New York he met the Baxter family. Sally, the eldest daughter, enchanted the novelist—as a number of vibrant, intelligent, beautiful young women had done before her—and she became the model for Ethel Newcome. He visited her on his second tour of the States when she was married to a South Carolina gentleman. His choosing of married women in the shape of both Jane and Sally was ill-advised and both relationships led nowhere but did take quite some time to disassemble and for reason to set in.

In 1852, The History of Henry Esmond was published as a 3-volume novel without first being serialised and in a special type meant to imitate the appearance of an eighteenth-century book. This was the most carefully planned of Thackeray's novels. The book was celebrated for its brilliance, and Thackeray recognized it as "the very best I can do". At the time, it caused a sensation thanks to its controversial ending, wherein the hero marries a woman who early in the novel seemed more like a "mother" to him.

The eighteenth-century held a great attraction for Thackeray and he had previously set both Barry Lyndon and Catherine there as well as the sequel to Esmond, The Virginians, which takes place in North America and includes George Washington as a character.

Thackeray had twice visited the United States on lecture tours during this period as well as given lectures in London on the English humorists of the eighteenth century, and on the first four Hanoverian monarchs. The latter were published in a book as The Four Georges.

Interestingly Thackeray also decided that Politics was something he could more than dabble in. In Oxford he stood as an independent for Parliament. He was narrowly beaten by Cardwell, a politician who was substituted for the man Thackeray thought he was going to run against, although Thackeray's advocacy of entertainment on the Sabbath would have done little to help his campaign. Even so the margin of his defeat was only 1,070 votes, to Thackeray's 1,005.

In 1860 Thackeray became editor of the newly established Cornhill Magazine, a role he never felt truly comfortable in, preferring to contribute as a columnist on the Roundabout Papers. However, the financial compensation was by all accounts quite extraordinary. The Cornhill began its history with a record circulation and a number of distinguished contributors swayed onboard by Thackeray's reputation. It was in the Cornhill that he serialised his last complete novel, The Adventures of Philip in 1861-62. (After his death, the incomplete Denis Duval would also appear there in 1864).

After two years as editor he stepped down, primarily to concentrate on writing novels again. A piece he wrote for the Cornhill at this time "Thorns in the Cushion," one of The Roundabout Papers, fondly assembles the pains he felt in rejecting manuscripts on the one hand and receiving criticism of the magazine on the other. It seemed a good time to move on.

Thackeray's health had worsened during the 1850s and he was plagued by a recurring stricture of the urethra that laid him up for days at a time. He also felt that he had lost much of his creative impetus. He worsened matters by excessively eating and drinking, and avoiding exercise, though he enjoyed horseback-riding. He has been described as "the greatest literary glutton who ever lived". Indeed, his main activity apart from writing was eating and drinking and many of his stories include elaborate scenes and themes on his fondness for them.

On December 23rd, 1863, William Makepeace Thackeray, after returning from dining out and before dressing for bed, suffered a massive stroke. He was found dead on his bed the following morning. He was only fifty-two.

His death was entirely unexpected, and shocked family, friends and indeed the entire Nation.

It is said that at his funeral service thousands of mourners turned out to witness his passing. He was buried on December 29th at Kensal Green Cemetery, London.

William Makepeace Thackeray – A Concise Bibliography

The Yellowplush Papers (1837)
Catherine (1839–40)
A Shabby Genteel Story (1840)
Second Funeral of Napoleon (1841)
The Irish Sketchbook (1843)
The Luck of Barry Lyndon (1844)
Notes of a Journey from Cornhill to Grand Cairo (1846)
Mrs. Perkins's Ball (1846), under the name M. A. Titmarsh
Stray Papers: Being Stories, Reviews, Verses, and Sketches (1821-1847)

The Book of Snobs (1848)
Vanity Fair (1848)
Pendennis (1848–1850)
Rebecca and Rowena (1850)
The Paris Sketchbook (1840)
Men's Wives (1852)
The History of Henry Esmond (1852)
The English Humorists of the Eighteenth Century (1853)
The Newcomes (1855)
The Rose and the Ring (1855)
The Virginians (1857–1859)
Lovel the Widower (1860)
Four Georges (1860-1861)
The Adventures of Philip (1862)
Roundabout Papers (1863)
Denis Duval (1864)
The English Humorists of the eighteenth century: A Series of Six Lectures (1867)
Ballads (1869)
Burlesques (1869)
The Orphan of Pimlico (1876)

Thackeray wrote a numerous number of articles for magazines and the like as well as contributing many picture sketches to articles and his own books. Many were then collected and published together. We have listed his major works only for this bibliography.